My Crime-Fighting Pet Skunk Is a Hero!

Adventure 2

Written and illustrated by Michelle Green

Secret Golden
Pages Press

Ordering Information: Special discounts are available on quantity purchases by corporations, associations, and others. For details, contact the publisher at the address above.

Editing and typesetting: Sally Hanan of www.inksnatcher.com
Cover design: Les of German Creative

My Crime-Fighting Pet Skunk Is a Hero!: Adventure 2/Michelle Green

ISBN
Paperback 979-8-9862511-4-1
Hardback 979-8-9862511-5-8
E-book 979-8-9862511-7-2
Audiobook 979-8-9862511-6-5

Printed in the United States of America.

I would like to dedicate my book to my wonderful daughter Tori Sloan, and all my amazing students!

You are all truly the best!

Chapters

1

My Teacher Is Green!

Crunch! Crunch! Squish! Lola stuffed Spike, her new pet skunk, down in her backpack to spend the day at school with her. Something metal and cold slid along his wet nose.

"This should be a wonderful day," mumbled Spike, who was now squished at the very bottom of her backpack. "Nothing more fun than spending a hot, sweaty day stuffed in Lola's smelly book bag," he complained again.

Lola danced with excitement and tossed her backpack up and down while she planned Spike's training.

"La la la la la," she sang as she spun in circles. Once they got to school, she threw Spike a treat or two into the bag each time the teacher wasn't looking.

Spike kept reaching around in the dark, trying to find what she kept throwing in. He slowly licked each snack to make sure they weren't something rotten or spoiled. To his surprise, they were quite tasty. He gobbled down treats all day long, not thinking about what kind of trouble it might cause. But by the end of the school day, he began to feel his belly starting to ache.

Spike's tummy began to rumble, tumble, and churn; and pressure began to build deep in his stomach. "Not again!" grumbled Spike. Without notice, he spewed a large spray of greasy skunk spray right through the backpack. *Poof.* It spewed everywhere.

It went right through the material like it was paper and spread all over the classroom. Through a small hole, Spike could see a fine, green mist floating through the air and quickly covering the teacher's hair.

Lola's teacher quit teaching in mid-sentence and suddenly couldn't speak anymore. She looked like a green ghost standing in front of the room. She started stuttering, and her nose started quivering up and down fast, while her top lip began to snarl like a dog. "Uh. Uh. Uh. Did something just die in here?" stuttered Lola's teacher finally. She grabbed her head and rubbed her eyes, up and down, hard. Spike could see little red veins starting to pop up in the whites of her eyes.

"Ahhhh!" A dozen students started screaming and tried to get out of their seats. Two students fell and their faces planted flat on the floor. Then three girls who were sitting right next to Lola froze in place, with their eyeballs open so wide, they looked like they were going to pop right out of their heads.

Then one of the boys who was making fun of another student stopped and forgot what he was going to say.

Lola didn't say a word. The spray floated through the air and even made its way down the hall to the principal's office before the teacher could even call for help.

"Evacuate, everyone, now! And I mean now! Something is seriously wrong!" snorted the principal through the loudspeaker. He sounded like a bull getting ready to trample everything in sight. Spike kept quiet as a mouse.

***

Students didn't follow their usual drill to leave the building. They ran as fast as they could, including Lola, tripping over everyone and screaming all the way through the halls. Lola ran with them, pretending she knew nothing. Books and backpacks flew everywhere.

The whole school left the building in a crazy mess in just a few seconds and piled on top of each other outside in the grass. No one even cared that they had forgotten to follow the rules. They just wanted to get some clean air. Hours went by as the students and teachers waited outside the school for a crew to attempt to get rid of the almost deadly smell.

Finally, Lola's bus pulled up, and she ran and jumped on the bus with no time to waste. She had to get Spike home before anyone found out she was the cause of this whole school emergency. She shuffled down the aisle searching for a seat and threw her bag with Spike in it on the floor. *Thud!*

"Oh, how I love being tossed to and fro," she heard him gripe.

Lola looked to the back of the bus and saw Simon, the coolest but rudest kid in school. It didn't make any sense that he was on the bus because he drove a race car to school every day, and never once did he set foot in any place that didn't look cool. He thought he was *so* fabulous. Lola gritted her teeth and thought about how mad he made her. His wavy, shiny hair and his polished look didn't impress her at all. He was only nice to the pretty girls and he ignored all the others. "What a fake," Lola grumbled. She sat down in an aisle seat and stared back at him, trying to figure out why he could possibly be on the bus.

"What are you looking at, little girl?!" he shouted. He stared so hard at her that it felt like his eyes pierced right through her. Lola felt her stomach drop and her heart start pounding. She stuck her head down quickly and looked quietly to the front of the bus without saying a word.

Lola wanted to say, "I'm looking at your ugly face," but decided that wasn't a good idea. At church, she'd learned if you didn't have something nice to say, it was best not to say anything at all. She'd also been taught to be kind to her enemies, so she took a deep breath and breathed out all her anger and breathed in as much relaxation as she could. Then she pulled out her note cards in her backpack with her Bible verses on them. Spike's footprints covered each card. *He must have been reading them all day while eating his treats*, she thought. "God did not give us a spirit of fear but of power, love, and a sound mind" (2 Timothy 1:7). Lola whispered it over and over again until she felt much better. She had a Bible verse for every problem, and she wasn't afraid to use them! Simon didn't matter to her anyway, as she had more important things to think about, and she couldn't wait to get Spike back into training.

"Yeah, that's right, little girl, keep your creepy face forwards and quit staring at me!" yelled Simon.

***

Spike heard every word, even though he was crunched down in the bottom of her backpack, and he became quite disgusted. He still felt pretty gassy, so his anger instantly released another small but deadly gas bomb that floated right to Simon's grumpy face.

As Spike watched through the hole, the tough, arrogant look on nasty Simon's face began to melt and turn into a look of complete disgust. He opened his mouth so far, Spike could see the back of his tonsils almost growing.

"Blaaaaaahhh!" Simon yelled as he pulled down the bus window and stuck his head out as far as he could. He hung his head over the side against the window and gasped for air. His tongue flapped in the wind as he tried to escape the smell. He breathed in three strong breaths of air and collapsed back down in his seat. His face was still showing total shock as he reached down and pulled his shirt up over his face. He stopped in mid-sniffle and gave a loud, strangled sound.

"Ewwwww!" screamed the whole bus full of students. They all thought the smell was coming from Simon, so they grabbed their noses and scooted to the front of the bus to get as far away from him as they could.

"Simon must have had a lot of beans for lunch!" yelled one of the boys, with a smirk on his face.

"He *is* pretty gassy," another kid said from a giggling group of kids in the front of the bus. Simon's cheeks turned red, and he slumped down in his seat so no one could see him.

The bus driver stomped on the brakes right in front of Lola's house and ran to the back of the bus with a can of air freshener.

Even though Spike's tummy still hurt, he laughed all the way out of the bus with a giggling Lola, through Lola's front door, and into her kitchen. He had a feeling Simon would not be riding the bus again anytime soon.

2

Spike Gets Cheesy CPR

Lola believed she had people to save with her new superhero called Spike, so she ran straight to the kitchen to make a fresh, hot, grilled cheese sandwich. She still had a strong appetite, even after sitting in a bus filled with Spike's strong, skunky smell.

After letting Spike out of her backpack, Lola turned the stove heat on and splashed butter all over the inside of her favorite blue frying pan.

Spike stumbled upstairs to get some rest after being stuffed in the backpack all day. He collapsed on the floor in Lola's room and fell fast asleep.

***

The butter on the stove heated up so fast that it started to bubble. Lola threw two pieces of bread in the sizzling butter and covered them with sharp cheddar cheese. The creamy cheese melted and oozed down the sides of the bread into the pan. Before it started to burn, she flipped the bread over with a spatula, pressed the two sides together, and threw it on a small plate. Then she grabbed a butter knife and cut her delicious sandwich into two triangles. It hadn't even cooled off before she started stuffing one of the pieces in her mouth. Hot cheese filled her cheeks and ran all over her tongue. Her mouth fried a little from the heat, but she still opened her mouth to take another giant bite. It was way too hot, but she kept on chewing. Then she reached down and grabbed her book bag and ran upstairs.

"Spikey! Where are you?" she yelled. She stepped into her room and looked down and saw Spike lying flat on the floor on his face. He was as still as a statue. "Oh no! Are you dead?" Lola panicked and jumped down to the floor. *Thud!* She grabbed him and rolled him onto his back and started blowing big puffs of air into his small, furry cheek. Spike opened his eyes in an instant and lay there looking stunned as she dropped hot cheese on his fur.

"WHY ARE YOU BLOWING HOT CHEESE ON MY FACE!" he yelled, his eyes stretched wide in shock. His face began to turn red, and Lola almost saw smoke coming out of his ears.

"My crime-fighting hero is not allowed to die," she cried out loudly, a chunk of cheese stuck on her top tooth. She grinned ear to ear, feeling joy deep in her heart because she was using her CPR training she had just taken the month before. "There is nothing more exciting than saving a life!" she yelled with joy.

***

Spike looked at Lola with a mean glare and tried to stretch his face as far as he could in the other direction. His efforts were wasted because she just kept blowing sizzling cheese all over him. Spike was so relieved she didn't know how to give *real* CPR or his mouth would have been filled with squishy cheese. He didn't have enough energy to try and escape because he was too sore and tired from all his skunk training.

"Yuck! Bluck!" said Spike. He began to taste a small chunk of cheese that had accidentally flown into his mouth. "Blahhhhh!" Spike yelled. "Blaaaahhh! Patoooey!"

He threw his head from side to side and slimy cheese flew out of his fur and stuck right into the fibers in the carpet. Spike could even feel a big chunk right on top of his ear. "Gross!!" He stuck his tongue out and yelled in a sharp skunk language, "STOP! YOU MANIAC! STOP BLOWING HOT SLIMY CHEESE ALL OVER MY FUR!"

Lola looked so happy. "Oh, thank goodness, Spike! You're alive! I knew I could save you!"

Spike stared at her, stunned. He wiped at his chin and felt some thick, yellow cheese sticking to his furry belly. He sat up covered in cheese and tried to figure out how this silly girl thought she had somehow saved his life. *It's more like she tried to kill me!* he thought. *Doesn't she know she is supposed to try to wake someone up before she gives them CPR?*

Spike began to hope it might just all be a bad dream, but he could still feel something slimy and mushy near the corner of his eye. This was worse than the time he fell in the toilet headfirst when she was trying to put him in another one of her ugly outfits. He began to stick his tongue out just to make sure no more cheese had flown inside his mouth.

"Oh, look at you! You are enjoying my yummy cheese, Spikey. I don't think skunks are supposed to eat cheese though. You can enjoy that cheese this time, but I am not giving you anymore," lectured Lola.

"What! Are you crazy? I'd rather eat one of your stinky shoes!" sneered Spike. "I wouldn't want any more of this squishy cheese if you stuck it on a grilled steak!" Spike glared at her, extreme anger in his belly.

"Well, now that I saved your life and shared my delicious grilled cheese with you, we can get back to training," Lola said happily, and she threw the last piece of hot grilled cheese in her mouth.

"Oh, goody gumdrops," Spike said sarcastically and grumbled while he tried to wipe the rest of the sticky mess off his chin and scooted behind the dresser to hide.

3

A Scary, Slimy Snake!

"Where are you?" Lola found and grabbed Spike and ran outside to the back pasture behind the house. The dry grass swayed in the breeze. She gazed at all the cow trails stretching in every direction and picked her favorite one, and then headed toward it with Spike under her arm.

"What a treat. We get to spend another day outside in the hot sun, tromping around," Spike grumbled. He could feel beads of sweat forming above his eyebrows and running sideways into his ears. Lola began to skip and sing, when suddenly she skidded to a quick stop. Instantly, dust and rocks flew everywhere, and one hit him right between the eyes. His eyes crossed, and Spike felt like they switched places. He rubbed his head and tried to straighten his eyeballs out. Soon, everything slowly came back into focus, and that's when he saw it—a giant, ugly snake with beady eyes slithering right behind a big tree into the dry grass.

"Ahhhhh!" yelled Spike as Lola headed straight for him with her arms stretched out wide.

"Woohoo! It's a bull snake!" screamed Lola in excitement. She ran closer, grabbed him by the tail, and threw him up through the air. He slithered sideways and tried to bite her right on the shoulder. "You're as cute and cuddly as Spike," Lola laughed.

"That thing is definitely not cuddly, and he is far from cute," Spike said, horrified.

Lola reached around and grabbed the snake by the neck, who was holding his mouth tight. "Boy, oh boy, I can't wait to show you to my friends!" Lola giggled.

Spike's stomach jumped as the snake tossed from side to side and hit him over the head again and again with his long, thick tail. Spike's fur began to stick up everywhere from each slap. His heart was about to pound right out of his chest as he tried to dodge the slithering snake.

Lola began to talk to the snake in a joyful tone of voice. "We will name you Freddy," Lola said laughing.

"Great. Now we named the scary, slimy thing," Spike said in an annoyed voice.

Lola ran back to the house and tumbled upstairs to her parents' bedroom, carrying the snake in one hand and Spike in the other. She slipped through the bathroom door and threw the giant bull snake in her dad's bathtub.

"There you go, snakey. You stay here while I go get a snacky-snack. She stuffed Spike under her armpit and ran downstairs.

Spike had a stomachache from being carried next to a creepy snake so long. Lola ate her snacky-snack and somehow forgot all about her new pet snake. She grabbed Spike and headed outside for another adventure.

***

About that time, Lola's dad came home from work and headed to his bedroom to take a nice, long, hot bath. "I can't wait to soak all my problems away," her dad said happily. His eyes were heavy and blurry from working on the computer all day long. He rubbed them up and down and reached around and turned on the hot water. Then he tossed a cup of bubble bath in quickly, from a distance, and headed back into his room to grab his blue bathrobe.

The giant snake was curled up right at the bottom and almost took up the whole tub. Snakey was not real happy about the bubbles and hot water.

Lola's dad made his way back into the bathroom slowly. "There is nothing like a hot bath after a long, hard day's work," he said to himself with happiness. Bubbles had formed and they covered the snake completely and oozed over the sides of the tub.

Dad jumped in the tub swiftly, and the soft bubbles surrounded him and caressed his back and toes. "So nice and relaxing," he sighed. Suddenly, something with a dark head and deep-red, beady eyes popped up from under the bubbles and stared him right in the face. Dad's mouth dropped opened wide, and his eyes almost popped out of his head.

Snakey looked like he was snarling, and his forked tongue slipped in and out at least a hundred times in just seconds. Lola's dad was so shocked he couldn't speak, and he froze in place for a second. Finally, he screamed "AHHHHHHHHHHHHHH!" like a little toddler, and he quickly tried to escape. He grabbed the side of the tub and attempted to jump out, but he slipped and landed right on top of Freddy.

The snake stuck his tongue out and his eyes turned from red to purple. He was already mad about the hot water and bubbles, but now he was beyond angry. He bit Lola's dad right on the rib—hard.

"Ahhhhhhhhhhhh!" Dad screeched, and bubbles flew everywhere. The snake blew bubbles out his nose and bit Dad again right on the back of the neck. Dad grabbed his neck and rib and slipped sideways out of the tub onto the floor.

He sounded like he did a belly flop when he hit the tile. It was so slippery that he slid all the way across the bathroom floor into the toilet plunger, which had just been used to unclog a huge toilet mess earlier. He could feel something sticky on his elbow and found toilet paper stuck to his arm, and he panicked and threw the plunger up in the air.

He started sloshing around on the floor and then finally grabbed the sides of a cabinet to try and pull himself up when Freddy slithered right underneath him. Dad gasped for air and jumped so high that he flew right into the sink with one loud *plop*.

"Lola!" he yelled. He knew this was another caper from her, but yet again, he couldn't prove it because she was nowhere to be found. The sink started coming apart from the wall and Dad found himself about to fall to the floor.

***

Meanwhile, Spike had just snuck in to try and hide from Lola when he heard Lola's dad screaming. He knew it had to be because of Lola's new, creepy pet. He grabbed a pillowcase from Lola's room and headed upstairs. "I'll get rid of that creepy critter," he said smugly. "I'm not planning on cuddling with that thing tonight."

Spike snuck upstairs and peeked into the bathroom. He could see Lola's father about to fall to the floor, sink and all. He threw the pillowcase out and held it right up against the door opening. Just then Freddy slithered right out the door into his trap. "Gotcha!" Spike cheered. He tied the end of the pillowcase, and snakey whipped around like a wild animal trying to escape.

"You are going far away to a land unknown," Spike announced. He pulled hard and dragged the monster downstairs, hitting the stair posts one at a time as the snake jerked and pulled. "I know what that feels like," said Spike. He looked at the front door and saw the garbage truck backing in to pick up the trash. "Perfect timing!" cheered Spike. He felt a quick burst of energy and he flew out the door faster than a chicken in a fox hunt, then started swinging Freddy in a circle as fast as he could and let go.

Freddy flew through the air and landed right in the back of the trash truck on top of an old couch. He stuck his shifty head out and then crawled inside one of the soft cushions. He was off to the dump.

"And there you go! No more pet snake!" howled Spike.

***

Lola's dad shook hard and hung tightly to the tipping sink for fifteen more minutes before he finally let go and started searching for his clothes. He covered his large fang bites with cream and slipped on his tall cowboy boots. He grabbed a large net and slowly and carefully began to search every inch of the house for Freddy. He hunted for hours, but he couldn't find the giant snake anywhere. He pulled out a pad and paper and wrote a new safety procedure down for the bathroom.

CHECK TUB FOR SNAKES!

He wrote in bright red letters. He taped the note to the wall next to the tub and then headed downstairs for something to eat. All that hard work was stressful and had made him really hungry. He rubbed his eyes again but didn't even think about taking a nap. He was afraid Freddy might crawl into bed with him, and he definitely didn't want to snuggle with him again. Thanks to Spike, the house was actually safe and snakeless, which he would soon discover.

4

Where's Spike's Other Leg?

To Spike's dismay, Lola came back into the house soon after her time in the back pasture, grabbed Spike by the paw, and dragged him into her mom and dad's room. "You are going to learn to move quick as a race car inside buildings," yelled Lola.

But race cars don't move in buildings! thought Spike, feeling alarmed.

Lola galloped around in her parents' bedroom. Spike watched her looking at all the furniture they could jump around on, and then she put both hands around his belly and swung her hands as low as she could towards the carpet. Then she threw him as high as she could through the air above her parents' bed. Spike almost hit the ceiling fan and then landed with a loud *thump* on the floor!

The skunk yelled in terror. "Ahhhhhhhh!" He smashed his lips together until he couldn't feel them and looked around in shock. He felt really dizzy but tried to look healthy and alive. He didn't want her to give him another round of CPR, and he definitely didn't want another mouthful of rotten-tasting cheese. "You're nuts!" he screamed.

That wasn't the end of it either. Lola pulled out a bag and looked inside the bag and then looked at Spike.

Oh goody. This should be another great *surprise,* he thought to himself.

Lola quickly stuffed him into the bag—she squashed him into it in a ball and left one of his legs sticking out of the bag.

"Where's my other leg?" he said angrily, his skunk paws trying to reach out through the top of the back to pull it in.

He felt Lola throw him over her shoulder, his hind leg hanging over her ear and his eyes peeking out the top in terror, and bounced against her as she started running around the room and jumping from one piece of furniture to another. She swooped onto the dresser and stepped on her dad's remote control to the TV. *Crunch!* It broke right in half, and a few sharp pieces fell into her dad's shoes. Next, she jumped from the dresser to an open drawer and knocked over a bottle of perfume. It poured all over her dad's briefcase next to the bed.

Spike bounced from side to side and did tumbles and circles in the bag as they flew around the room. It was just like riding one of the scariest carnival rides ever, but now he'd fallen back into the bag and couldn't see a thing. The only thing he could see were stars flying around his head from getting bumped over and over again.

"Now, one more training for the day and you will be done!" yelled Lola as she pulled him out of the bag.

"Woohoo!! That is so *not* wonderful," grumbled Spike.

"All you need is your helicopter training!" Lola said happily.

Oh, turkey fritters! thought Spike. *What could she possibly mean by helicopter training?* In his little skunk heart, he knew it had to be bad, and he wished he could be anywhere else but there.

Lola left for a moment and then came back into the room dragging a tall, silver ladder with something gray hanging over her shoulder.

"Yikes!" screamed Spike. A small dust cloud formed in the air as she scraped the ladder through the carpet fibers across the floor and stopped right below the ceiling fan. Spike gulped as she grabbed him and strapped a grey bag over his shoulders.

"Chicken feathers! I was right! This is not good at all!" he cried.

Next, Lola threw him back in her bag, this time with both his legs inside it, and headed up the ladder. The steel steps crunched as she made her way high up the ladder, all the way to the ceiling. *Crunch! Crunch! Crunch!* At the very top, she reached out and set him right on top of one of the smooth, brown blades on her parents' ceiling fan in the middle of their room.

Spike looked down and lost his breath from the fear of dropping to the floor. He could taste dirt in his mouth from all the dust built up on the top of the fan blade, and he tried to balance himself and keep from falling. *This was definitely not the skunk life I had hoped to live,* he thought as he stared at the long drop to the floor.

"Sit still," Lola told him as she started climbing back down the ladder and left him up there.

Sit still? There is nowhere to go. I couldn't move a muscle if I wanted to, he thought. *Where does she think I am going to go?* He knew if he took one step, he would splatter on the floor. His legs froze in place and his muscles began to ache from fear of moving. Somehow, Spike knew nothing good could come from this.

Lola's steps back down the ladder echoed in his head and seemed to go in very slow motion. He held his breath and closed one eye while he sat there, frozen in time, watching her. His legs began to shake.

"Don't worry, Spike. Your parachute will stop your fall!" she yelled up to him.

"Fall? Parachute? Yikes! Is that what this thing tied to me is? This might be it!" he stuttered. "Where are the days when everyone was scared of me?" he whispered with a shaky voice. "Where are the crowds running and screaming to escape my spray? I need Jesus to save me once again."

Spike wanted to close both eyes for the prayer, but he was much too scared to miss what Lola was up to, so he left one eye open and cringed his teeth while he watched her every move. "Dear Jesus, protect my bones from any breakage!" he yelped.

Ahh! Are you trying to kill me?

Yay!

When Lola got to the bottom of the ladder, she headed straight for the fan switch. He was about to let out a skunk scream, but before he knew it, she'd flipped the switch and he was flying in circles around the room so fast that everything became one, big, foggy blur. He dug his nails deep on the fan blade, but his claws began slipping slowly down the wooden rectangle. It made a loud screeching noise, like fingernails on the chalkboard.

The parachute Lola had attached to Spike's back was making it even harder to hold on. It had formed an air pocket and was pulling him backwards towards the wall. He was so scared, he could no longer hold it in, and he started spewing wet, smelly gas all over the room.

***

Skunk spray flew everywhere! The whole room was glossed over with a strong, greasy mist in just seconds! Lola was so surprised, her mouth dropped open, and some skunk spray flew right in. When she looked in her mom's mirror, she could see her face had turned a dark, moldy green. The greasy mist made her taste buds go numb right after she tasted the grossest taste she ever tasted in her life.

"Bluck!" Lola blurted out. She coughed over and over again and then wiped her face with her sleeve and acted as though nothing happened.

***

Sammy breathed in one snort of the smell in the air and it made him fall over flat on his back. He almost looked dead, but that was only for a short second. He opened both eyes wide and tried to look perfectly fine, so he didn't get Lola's special CPR he saw her give to Spike. Then he pulled his ears over his eyes and nose and tried to protect himself from the smell.

Spike looked like he was barely hanging on by his paws when he spewed another giant puff of wet, gassy spray all over the ceiling again, and across the room into the bathroom! Sammy could almost see a rainbow in the room because the air was so wet.

***

Finally, Lola knew Spike could no longer hold on. His nails had scraped through the top of the fan blade to the very end, chipping off several pieces of wood. As she watched, he flew off it and across the room at high speed and hit the wall. *Splat!* He stuck to the wall as flat as a pancake, froze to it for a moment, and then he slowly skidded down the side of the wall, making a high-pitched screeching noise all the way down to the baseboards. It was just like in the cartoons on TV.

"All righty, Spikey! Boy, do you know how to fly!"

***

Spike could feel his lower lip begin to fatten and puff up, and a gigantic bump was growing above his eyebrow. His face felt crooked now, and one ear felt a little lower than it had been before.

"Oh, poor Spikey! Your face is a little beat up now." Lola said as she smooched him. "I will take care of you! I don't have any gauze, but I know a special secret to bandage you all up!"

"Oh boy! Just what I need—another first aid treatment from Lola," Spike grumbled.

Lola grabbed a huge roll of toilet paper and began to run around him singing, "I'll be comin' around the skunky when I come!"

She sang it over and over again while she ran around him in circles at least fifty times. She didn't stop until Spike was completely covered in toilet paper with just the tip of one ear hanging out. "There you go, Spikey! All taken care of! You will be good as new in just a few hours!"

Spike couldn't see a thing inside his toilet paper prison. He stuck out one claw and poked a couple of holes in the paper so he could see. "Okay, that is it. This toilet paper thing is the last straw!" he declared. "This is much worse than the pink dress," he murmured. "I am going to make an escape tomorrow if it is the last thing I do. No more training and no more Lola!"

5

I Need More Soap!

Lola's dad was eating a snack in the kitchen when he started to smell something strong coming through the vents. "BLAHHHH! What is that smell?!" yelled her dad in a loud, deep voice. He could no longer eat because the smell was getting stronger and thicker in the air. His applesauce started to taste like he'd dipped it in a sewer, and his cheeks began to quiver. "Yuck!" he shouted. He spat his snack in the trashcan and began to stomp around the house to try and see what was going on. He could taste something really bad in the air, and his nose was starting to burn.

Lola's dad went from room to room until the odor got stronger and stronger. He finally found where the smell was coming from. It was coming from his room!

"OH NO!" yelled her father. He had a feeling Lola had to have had something to do with the mess before his eyes, but he couldn't prove it. He never could. He always just saw the mess after she was gone. He ran inside his room and the smell made his eyes start running streams of water that dripped onto his shirt. He looked like he was crying.

Lola and her skunk were already gone, and when he looked out the window, he could see them relaxing outside in the front yard. He knew the powerful fumes had to be Lola's fault.

Dad reached for his glasses on the dresser and grabbed them, but they were all wet and covered in some kind of sticky spray. The strong smell parted his nose hairs. He tried to rub his glasses clean, but they just smeared even worse. He put them on anyway and then quickly slipped on his shoes.

Crunch! He felt something stuck in the side of his foot in his shoe, like a small dagger. "Ahhhhhh," he yelled. Though he could barely see a thing though his filthy glasses, he could see pieces of his TV remote control sticking in the heel of his foot. "Ouchy Mama!" he yelled again.

Dad hobbled into the bathroom and grabbed his toothbrush to try and get the taste out of his mouth. He was happy to see there was already toothpaste on his toothbrush, so he stuck it right in his mouth and started brushing quick and fast. But what was on his tongue wasn't toothpaste at all! It was a big ball of something wet and gross that smelled like nothing he had ever smelled before! "OH NO!

BLAHHHHHHH!" he yelled. He spat all over the bathroom trying to get the taste out.

Suddenly, he slipped and fell headfirst into the toilet. *Splash!* Toilet water flew all over him and covered his hair and shirt completely. He slung his arm back and then tons of water from the commode hit the wall. Stinky skunk spray and yucky toilet water ran down his shirt and pants, and his tongue was numb and sticky! "Ahhhhh!" he yelled again.

Dad squinted his eyes and tried to see through his greasy glasses, scooting up close to the mirror to see his wet hair, but all he could see was something brown and sticky in it. He didn't even want to think what that might be, but thought it actually couldn't be much worse than what he had just tasted and smelled in his mouth. He was beginning to wish he could go back to the day he was chasing the fat jelly bug and only had jelly in his hair.

Dad checked the bathtub for snakes and then quickly jumped in and started pouring liquid soap all over himself. He scrubbed so hard that bubbles flew everywhere. He grabbed shampoo, shower gel, hair rinse, hand sanitizer, bathtub cleaner, and anything else he could get his hands on. Even though he knew all this soap was probably not too healthy mixed together, he was desperate to get rid of the smell.

He disappeared into the bubbles and he scrubbed and scrubbed, but the smell was stubborn. It hung on to him like a tic on a dog. "That's it!" he yelled. He rinsed off the bubbles with the showerhead, dried off, and went straight to the internet to search for help.

Dad's hair stuck straight up on his head as he looked up all the companies that could tackle toxic smells. His now crooked, soapy eyebrows sparkled in the light from scrubbing them so hard. He finally found just the right place and begged them to come over right away. While he was waiting for them to get there, he decided to relax, so he sat down and grabbed his computer to get some work done.

He tried to open the screen up and it barely opened. He could feel something dry and sticky on it, and it seemed heavy. Once he got it open enough, he could see something purple and gummy-like all over the screen and keys. It looked like grape jelly but smelled, oddly, like really strong perfume.

"Lola! Have you been using my computer?!" he yelled. He knew she wasn't there, and he knew what the answer was without her even saying a word. He had to yell to get his stress out though. He looked at the hard jelly between the keys and he felt like smoke was coming out of his nose and ears. He breathed deeply and calmed down and relaxed. *It was just an old computer. I had everything backed up anyway. But all my computers will be under lock and key from now on*, he thought.

Men in special suits showed up quickly and spent the rest of the day scrubbing every inch of the house. The tall, slender man asked what happened, but Lola's father had no answers. He actually didn't want to know.

It was a long day, but when Lola's mom got home, everything was spick and span, so he didn't have to tell her about how he took a bubble bath with a snake, fell in the toilet, and ate something toxic.

Lola somehow escaped getting into trouble once again, and she got to keep her crime-fighting pet skunk for another day.

6

More Superhero Training for Spike

Spike was determined to escape, but he had no energy to try and get away that night because Lola had worn him out. His arms felt like they were six inches longer after being stretched as far as they could go when he was flying in circles on the fan. His arms lay like spaghetti on the bed, and he couldn't move them anywhere. He stared at them lying there lifelessly until he finally fell asleep.

The next morning, Lola dragged him out of bed even earlier than the day before—at 3 a.m.! There was just no break from his army work. His training was so rough that one ear was hanging and his left eyebrow was now bigger than a baseball. Apparently, Lola believed there was no time to rest when they were going to save the world.

On their way down the stairs, Lola got Spike's tail stuck under her foot, which sent them both tumbling to the bottom of the staircase together. *Wham! Bam! Thud!* Spike could feel his cheek hit the rails at least five times!

"Oopsy! But you're okay. Spikey, you are going to have such a fun day today again!"

Oh goody. More training. and so nice and early.

"Woo. Hoo. Another fun-filled day," mumbled Spike, while he wondered if he still had all his body parts. He couldn't quite figure out when she thought he'd had a fun day. He also was hoping they could at least make it down or up the stairs just once safely.

They finally made it outside and she set him in the sandbox. "Okay, Spike! I want you to do one hundred push-ups, fifty windmills, seventy-eight sit-ups, and two hundred jumping jacks right now!" she yelled.

Spike stared back at Lola with an evil glare and wondered how that was even possible. He didn't move a muscle because he didn't even know where to start with that big of a request. He didn't even know if he could move his spaghetti arms at all anymore. *Maybe, I should start on the first push-up and try to get them over with,* he thought, but he wasn't even sure if he could do one push-up, let alone one hundred.

Lola pulled out her whistle and blew it hard. There was no time to think. His ears were ringing, so he just started jumping up and down over and over again, doing jumping jacks instead. His cheeks started flapping back and forth and high and low. He could feel his mouth fill up with pockets of air while he tried to catch his breath.

Spike hoped Lola might forget about the hundred push-ups, but he knew that probably would not happen. Sweat poured off his head, ran down his furry cheeks, and dripped into the dirt. Up, down, up, down, up, down. He never knew he could do that many exercises in such a short amount of time.

Spike tried to plan out an escape in between his exercises. He got to the push-ups last, and there was no energy left for him to lift his little skunk body. He went down and stayed down. It felt so good to lie there, flat in the dirt, that he almost wanted to kiss the ground.

Lola blew her whistle again loudly. "I want to see those push-ups *now*!" she yelled. "Only ninety-nine more to go!" Spike gulped hard. He didn't know how he could possibly do even one more, let alone one hundred. He took a deep breath and pressed his paws firmly in the dirt. He pushed with all his might and his claws pressed into the soft dusty ground. Nothing moved; he was still flat on the ground with his muscles sagging so low, they were dragging around in the dirt.

"Don't be a quitter!" Lola yelled again at the top of her lungs. "You can do this! Let me show you how!" she shouted and jumped down in the dirt. Dust flew everywhere when she hit the ground, and it almost looked like a whirlwind around her. Spike waved his paw in front of his face to get the dust out of his eyes. Then Lola put her hands flat on the ground and pushed hard. She grunted and blew air through her nose, but nothing happened. She didn't move an inch. She breathed in deeply, tried one more time, and let out an even louder grunt. Nothing happened again, and her face started to turn purple. Spike smirked and started to laugh a quiet skunk laugh.

"Well, maybe a hundred is a little much," she said with a sigh. We can cut that back to ONE. So you're done, Spike! Great job!"

Whew! That was close! Spike thought. He was so happy, he jumped up, but he jumped way too fast because he fell right back over in the dirt. His muscles were completely used up.

Lola scooped him up and took him upstairs and threw him in bed, and then she left him alone. That was the only thing he liked about the whole day.

Spike Is a Hero!

Spike made sure he didn't sleep too hard, so that he didn't look dead and get another round of CPR when Lola came home. He was super happy she thought he did well in her Air Force training because he didn't want to go for another ride on the ceiling fan either. Lola had seemed to think his flight, when he slammed into the wall, was perfect. Maybe, it was the fact his face was still crooked, or maybe it was because she got a mouthful of skunk spray. Spike wasn't sure, but he was super glad he didn't have to do that all over again.

7

An Escape Goes All Wrong

Several days went by until Spike finally got his chance for a possible escape. In the middle of the night, he slowly pulled loose from Lola's grip and was able to squeeze out from under her arms and sneak out the bedroom door.

This is finally it! Spike thought. "I am going to finally be free! No more exercises," he whispered. He tiptoed out the bedroom door on his little skunk tippytoes and into the hallway. Peeking from side to side, he crept slowly to the top of the staircase. He looked straight down the stairs and he could see the large, wooden front door ready for him to walk on to his freedom. He pictured himself fully escaped and sunbathing on the beach at Elephant Butte Lake, eating hotdogs out of the trash cans in total luxury.

All of sudden, before he could begin his journey, he heard a loud noise in the kitchen. It startled him so bad, he jumped backwards and hit the wall. His heart pumped so hard that he scurried into the laundry room and jumped into the first open door he could find, which just happened to be the dryer. *This is the perfect hiding place*, he thought. He nestled into the soft, warm clothes and decided to wait until he thought the coast was clear. He yawned and got so comfortable that before he knew it, he was almost sound asleep. It was such a relief not to have to listen to Lola's loud snoring in his ear that somehow, he forgot all about his plans to escape. He stretched out in complete happiness in the soft, fluffy clothes and curled his furry feet into a thick, silky pajama shirt. He dreamed wonderful dreams for three, full, straight hours.

However, morning came too soon and brought it all to a quick ending. Out of the blue, something wet and heavy hit him right smack in the face. Lola whistled happily and threw a giant handful of wet clothes right on top of him.

"Hmmm. Let me see. Where is the hottest setting? Oh, here it is! Extra hot and fluffy!" She hit the Start button and headed out the door.

Before Spike even saw her leave, he was flipping back and forth, up and down, and around and around in circles with flaming-hot air blowing up his tail. "Ahhhh!" he screeched. *Thud! Bang! Bam! Wham!*

***

Lola's mom could hear several loud crashes from her bedroom and decided to look into it. It was only a week ago when she'd found a whole bookbag with books, a candy bar, and bottled water in the dryer. She didn't want to have to try and clean up another chocolate mess again. She walked into the laundry room and slowly opened the dryer door to see what might be the problem. She bent over and looked deep into the dryer, and there in the back of the dryer was Spike, sitting up in the middle of the pile of clothes, with all his fur sticking straight up.

"Oh! You poor little skunky you! How did you get in there?" Mom said softly.

"Bad getaway plan," he slurred with smoke coming out his ears.

"I'm so happy I heard you tumbling around in there!" Mom said sweetly. She carefully wrapped him in her arms and pulled him out of the hot dryer. She quietly walked him to Lola's room and laid him gently on her bed. She tried to pat his hair down, but every time she tried, it just stood right back up. She sighed and left him on the bed to recover.

***

"Well, that escape went really wrong," Spike grumbled. He grabbed Lola's hair gel off her dresser and slicked his fur back into place. He had no idea what a dryer was, but there was no question it was something he NEVER wanted to jump back in again.

Spike walked by the mirror to see if his fur was burnt because he thought he smelled something and there was smoke coming out from under his feet. He looked closely in the mirror for any signs of fire and noticed his biceps were getting larger and his quads were looking a little more buffed. He flexed his right skunk arm in the mirror and admired his new bodybuilding look. He was the buffest skunk he'd ever seen.

Spike moved his arms left and right and took a look at all his new muscles. He stuck his chest out and held his head high. *I am definitely crime-fighting material*, he thought as he admired himself. He pictured himself as an FBI agent chasing down criminals on TV. "Hmmmm. This might work after all," he whispered to himself.

8

The Pet-Napper

Saturday came, and now it was time for Lola to see if there were any other cases for her and Spike to solve. Lola had talked to her best friend at school on Friday, but the only problem her friend had was a missing pencil, and people lose their pencils all the time, so that wasn't really a true crime. It was only a crime in Lola's eyes if the pencil had one of those special animal erasers. "Time to search for more crimes," Lola said to herself.

Lola decided to visit her neighbor, who was also a great friend of hers. Her name was Sally Girl. She was tall and thin with short, black hair. Sally Girl always dressed so beautifully that everyone put the word "girl" after her name, so her name became Sally Girl.

Sally Girl was fun to hang out with because she was so creative. She helped Lola build amazing things because she could reach almost anything and build tall inventions. Not only that, but she was an amazing decorator. She mixed all the right colors together and added all the right things to anything they built. She could make a cardboard box look like a castle!

Lola knocked on the door and Sally Girl came tromping up. *Boom!* She threw open the door and hugged Lola tightly. Lola felt like she got the stuffing squeezed right out of her, but she felt very loved.

"Are you here to build a new invention?"

"No, I'm sorry. I am actually looking for a crime to fight in the area," said Lola. She pulled up her collar and tried to look like she was a real detective looking for a suspect.

Sally Girl looked impressed. She thought for a moment and then told Lola about a pug named Ralph that had been stolen just up the street, and a giant, forty-pound turtle named Jewel, who lived around the corner, and who had also disappeared.

"Jackpot!" Lola yelled and jumped quickly with excitement. She knew she could solve this case, easy-peasy! She gave Sally Girl another huge hug and ran off to start work on her first real detective case.

Lola knew that she would have to come up with some bait to catch this spooky pet-napper. "I'm going to catch this creeper soon!" yelled Lola. "What could be better than a pet skunk disguised as a pet cat for perfect bait!"

Lola started her plan by spreading news about her new, expensive, exotic pet. She planned on dressing him up and parading him around for all eyes to see. *Ohhh! What an amazing plan I have*, she thought. *This pet-napper is as good as caught!*

Lola waited a couple of days for the news of her pet to get around, and then when Friday came, she grabbed Spike and threw his dress back on. This time, she had to make him look a little more valuable, so she stuck her fancy pink, ruffled bow on top of his head too. Spike didn't seem thrilled with the dress, and his face told her that the ugly bow that covered his eyes was just going way too far. He seemed to say that this was just not the right kind of disguise for a tough, crime-fighting hero like himself, but Lola ignored him. Next, she grabbed her perfume and sprayed it right in his face.

"Whoa! Yuck!" complained Spike. He coughed several times and then started to sneeze, and then his snot started running all the way down the front of his disguise. A nose and a mouth full of perfume wasn't the best start to a crime-fighting day, but Lola didn't even notice all the fluid running out of his face because she was too delighted with his new smell. She breathed deeply and enjoyed the sweet perfume scent.

Once Lola thought he was ready, she grabbed him, tucked him under her arm, and ran out to the sidewalk. She began to skip up and down the block with him and sang, "I love my pet! La la la la la!" over and over again. Lola's voice was out of tune, and it was so loud, it almost echoed, but everyone knew she had a fancy, rare pet now.

Once she got back to the house, Lola blinked her eyes and licked the corner of her lip, thinking about how she was soon going to soon capture the pet-napper with her crime-fighting hero pet. She slid Spike's bow to the side and then put him in his special pink, fur crate in the front yard on top of a small table. Spike did not look happy about being stuck in a pink, fuzzy crate again and dressed in a pink dress with an ugly, pink bow on his head.

Lola reached down and clasped her hands together right next to the bars on the crate and said a prayer quietly with Spike. "Dear Jesus, please protect Spike and help us stop the pet-napper, in Jesus's name," she whispered. She knew if anyone could help her stop a pet-napper, it would be Jesus.

"Dear Jesus, protect me from Lola again today. Help me keep all my teeth and body parts. Amen!" Spike whispered.

Spike Is a Hero!

Lola looked up and down the street. She had her camera ready in her front pocket—just in case he or she showed up soon. She blew Jesus a kiss in the air and thanked him for helping her find Spike in the pet store. She told him she couldn't wait to see how he would help her stop the pet-napper. Then she hid quietly by the side of the house. She waited and watched for about two whole hours, but not much happened, so she walked back to Spike.

"This is how it works," she whispered to Spike. "You have to be patient and wait for the bad guy to show up, and then you tackle him."

***

Spike opened one eye and pretended to listen while he kept snoring away. He knew it might be his only chance for rest, and he wasn't going to give it up for anything.

As the day went by, two girls with pigtails wearing long, twin, blue dresses walked by and giggled as they peeked into his crate. Spike rolled over to the other side of the crate and ignored them. Then later, three boys on mountain bikes came by and rode in circles in front of him. Spike didn't care to talk to them either, so he flipped over again and kept on sleeping. Lola took pictures, just in case. The boys were just trying to get a good look at Spike to see what he was without looking like they were staring. They couldn't figure it out, so they went on their way too.

Not much else happened all morning. Spike loved this new sleeping job. He snored away on his back, on his stomach, and on his side. It was much too perfect. He started to hope they could spend a few weeks doing this type of work. He rested so well that he forgot all about his sweaty hours of training. Nothing could be any better. He could feel the warm sun on his nose as he dreamt off into another world. Late in the afternoon, everything changed for Spike though. His sleep was put to a complete stop and everything turned dangerous in just seconds.

***

Just when Lola thought the day was wasted, a guy with dark sunglasses pulled up in a maroon sports car and parked next to the curb. It was Simon! The boy from the school bus who had yelled at her on the way to school! *What in the world could he be doing here?* she wondered. *He definitely isn't here for a visit.* Simon never really spoke to that many kids, and if she did talk to him, most of the time he would just stare at her like she was strange or something. She remembered the cold, heartless look he had in his eyes from the bus. Then she thought about how he had almost knocked her over two or three times when he was walking down the

school hallway too. He quietly jumped out of the car and
grabbed Spike.

***

Spike didn't waste a second. He grabbed the bow out of his
fur and threw his disguise off, just like the superheroes did
in the movies. He didn't want to wait for Lola to help
because he wanted to keep all of his teeth. He'd actually
been waiting all day to get rid of that pink dress and the
ugly ruffled bow anyway. "I'm not going anywhere with
you," he muttered in skunk language.

Spike was just about to spray him when Simon grabbed his tail and threw him in a big bag. "Not another bag!" yelled Spike. He tried to break free by using his claws to scratch the inside of the bag, but he was stuck. His feet were bent all the way up to his face, and he couldn't move an inch. He slipped one foot up through the opening in the bag, and he could feel the air and the edge of the pet-napper's shirt with his toes, but it was too tight to fit the rest of his body through.

***

Luckily, Lola was prepared. She grabbed a bottle of water that she had dyed pink and threw it all over Simon's head.

"Pink! I'm all pink! What in the world is that?" panicked Simon. He tried to wipe the dreadful color off his face, but it only smeared his face more, and his hands and arms were covered in thick, bright slime that would not come off. He wiped it back and forth on his pant legs, but now it was on his clothes too. He couldn't think because all he could see was pink goop everywhere! Then all of a sudden, he felt Lola stick something sharp that felt like a gun in his back. It was just an empty water bottle, but he couldn't see it.

Spike Is a Hero!

"Freeze! Open the bag now, Simon!" shouted Lola. She was so loud, she surprised Spike, who accidentally released a squirt of skunk spray in the bag.

Simon froze and didn't move a muscle except for his nose muscles, which looked like they were having spasms and jumping everywhere. He scrunched his nose up and down, obviously trying to get rid of the awful smell.

Then Lola jabbed him harder in his spine. "Let the animal go or eat lead!" she yelled.

Simon looked left and then right, standing in complete shock. "Who are you? Where are you? How do you know my name?" He squinted his eyeball, scrunched up his nose again, and looked everywhere. "I'm usually so fast, no one is able to catch me. Please don't shoot!" And what is that DISGUSTING smell? Very puzzled, he slowly opened the bag, and Spike stuck the rest of his foot out of the opening and started making his way out. He'd almost made it all the way out of the bag when Simon stuffed him back in.

"This smell is far worse than any bullet! I'm out of here!" he yelled and made a run for it. He ran quickly, but it looked like the putrid odor was following him, and his eyeballs started to bob up and down.

"AHHHHH! Where is that awful smell coming from!" he screamed.

Lola grabbed her skateboard and went after him at full speed. Simon could hear her on his heels. Lola's wheels were spinning against the ground. Simon tried to pick up more speed, but the fumes from the bag were making him so dizzy, he started running crooked and flopping from side to side.

Lola skidded sideways, and sparks flew everywhere as her wheels slid on the ground right next to him. She could see Spike's foot sticking out through the top of the bag, so she jumped off the skateboard and landed right on top of Simon's arm. She put all of her weight on his elbow until she'd pulled the entire bag open.

Desperate to keep Spike, Simon reached down into the bag with his other hand to try and grab him. He grabbed something alright, but it wasn't furry and it didn't feel like a pet. It was something hot, soft, and mushy instead! It squished in between his fingers and started oozing all over his hand. It was skunk poop seeping underneath his fingernails!

"AAAAAAAAHHHHHHHHHH!" Simon shouted, as he stared at the mush all over his hand. "The smell is coming from this weird animal! How could this awful-smelling creature be worth any money?" he hollered at the top of his lungs. He could barely even hold the bag anymore.

Spike Is a Hero!

***

Spike crawled up the side of the bag, turned his tail straight up in the air, and blew three giant puffs of greasy gas right in Simon's face. *Poof! Poof! Poof!* The most toxic gas ever soared through the air right into Simon's nose.

"Aaaaaaaaaaaaahhhhhhhhhhhhhh!" Simon turned blue and dropped Spike right on his head. *Boing! Boing! Boing!*

"Ouch!" Spike shouted. He bounced right onto the street. *Boing! Boing! Boing!* It didn't bother him too much because Lola threw him around all the time, so he was pretty tough. His muscles in his neck tightened, and he bounced like a pogo stick until he stopped next to the curb. He got up off the road quickly and pulled a big, black stone out of his nose with his paw. "I'm free!" yelled Spike.

The pet-napper stood there in complete shock at what had just happened, holding his arm over his face and nose except for the times he was trying to get the taste out of his mouth. "Someone save me! Where is my car?" he cried. Finally, he reached out through the thick, cloudy gas and touched the door. He still had skunk poop all over his hand, so he tried to shake it off, but it only splattered all over his clothes. He grabbed the door handle, but his hand kept slipping because he couldn't get a grip on it with all the mushy skunk slime slipping around on his hand.

Lola kept snapping pictures while he wobbled around in a daze, but then all of a sudden, he turned yellow, fell right over, and splatted right on the street. The spunk poop was just too much for him to take. Spike had OVER-slimed and OVER-gassed the bad guy!

"Perfect!" cheered Lola. She ran into the house and dialed the police on her mom's cell phone.

Twelve minutes went by and then four shiny, black police cars came screeching up in front of the house. The pet-napper was a wanted man. He had been escaping the police for months and months. Spike and Lola caught him with one try! One police officer had his windows rolled down when he pulled up. His face turned from a cheery smile to a sickened, green, queasy look. He swiftly rolled up his windows and disappeared. "I've got another emergency call I have to go to!" he yelled over the radio as he drove off.

Another officer stepped out of his car, took one look at Simon, breathed the air in, and then got back into his car and sped off too. "I saw a wanted man just drive by. I have to go!" the second officer shouted over his radio.

Luckily, there were still two police cars left, but they were not in a rush to jump out of their cars. They called back to the station to check to make sure it was safe to get out because they could smell something really strong.

Officer Mike sat on his radio for about ten minutes talking about the extreme fumes, and then they all stepped out of the car. They carefully surrounded the pet-napper, but he wasn't moving.

"Wake up!" yelled Officer Mike.

The pet-napper still didn't move an inch.

"We're going to have to call in the paramedics!" yelled Officer Max.

They used their radios to call for help to revive him, and warned them to wear protective suits and gas masks.

The paramedics pulled up quickly, with lights flashing everywhere, and they looked like they were from another planet or called to land on the moon or something because they had special suits covering them from head to toe. They grabbed their gear and hooked a huge tank of oxygen up to Simon's mouth to try to wake him out of his faint. He was slobbering all over himself, and his lip was sagging sideways. He was mumbling something about his nose falling off.

"Wake up!" the doctor hollered in his ear.

The two officers shook him back and forth, sliding him across the gravel in the street. Then they grabbed a small little pouch and pinched some of the powder in it and dropped it into his nose. It must have been something strong because his eyes popped open and he started to scream.

"AHHHHH! Someone help me! My nose is about to explode!"

Police Officer Mike yelled to the other officers, "He is awake, but this guy stinks!" Then he began to gag.

"Yep! I have never arrested anyone who smelled this bad before. We may have to call the fire department to hose him off before we load him in our car!" said the shorter officer, coughing.

"I'm not loading him in my car!" yelled Officer Mike. He was choking. "That smell will melt the leather off my seats!"

"Maybe we can use the car we wrecked last week trying to stop the bank robbery."

"That is a great idea, if it still runs. All we need to do is get him to the jailhouse."

The fire department pulled up right next to them. "We got a call about a really bad smell in the area causing people to faint and call 9-1-1," said the firefighter. They all stared right at the pet-napper, who was out cold and covered in pink paint. "I'm guessing he is the problem," said Fireman Matt.

"Yes, he has a smell that is beyond horrible," complained the officer.

"Grab the hoses!" the firefighter yelled to the men on the truck. The firefighters pulled out their hoses and aimed them straight at the pet-napper. They knew he was the source of the toxic smell right away. They were about to spray all the water they had directly on him, but the firefighters' hoses instantly all went limp from the terrible odor.

"Give us a hand, officers!" shouted Fireman Matt. The police made their way over to help the firefighter. They grabbed the limp hose and cupped their hands tightly around it and held it out straight. Then they turned on the water and it gushed through the hose like a flood, hitting the pet-napper so fast, he flew backwards. Simon hit the wall hard, but he actually looked a little happier.

"Thank you, Mr. Fireman," he shouted above the sound of the rushing water.

Fireman Matt looked at him, stunned. "No one has ever thanked me for spraying them with a stream of water this fast before!" shouted the firefighter. After thirty minutes, they turned off the water to the hoses and started winding them in. The smell did not go away though. It slowly started to appear again, and it stuck to Simon like a magnet. It just would not wear off.

"We can't get rid of the smell!" yelled Fireman Matt. "We are going to load up and head out," he said as he headed toward the fire truck. "We are out of here!"

All the firefighters raced after him and were loaded in seconds. They couldn't wait to escape the area.

"The wrecked police car won't start, so we can't use it! But the captain says the rule book allows for transport on the roof of a regular car if the criminal is toxic," said Officer Mike.

"He is definitely toxic," stated Officer Max. He grabbed his thick gloves and began strapping Simon to the top of the police car. The pet-napper closed his eyes tight and his stomach felt queasy.

"Don't be scared. It will work great. I rode on top of the car when we went after the bank robbers last week, and it was no problem," explained the officer.

He started the cop car up and they headed off to jail. Simon breathed in the clean air blowing through his hair and nose and smiled. The smell that made his eyelashes curl was now flying away in the air. "Ahhhhhh!" the pet-napper sighed in relief. "Finally, a break from that horrible, awful smell!" He hung his head over the front window and his feet flopped back and forth in the air, leaving skunk smells everywhere on top of the police car. He smiled from ear to ear and breathed in deeply.

Officer Mike and his deputy both held one hand over their faces all the way to the jail because they didn't have the awesome breeze Simon had outside the car.

"I think I got some skunk spray on my sleeve," gurgled Officer Max. "It's worse than when I fell through the window into a room full of a hundred piles of dog poop when I was chasing that thief a few months ago."

"I think I got some skunk poop on my pocket," grumbled Officer Mike, looking at a brown spot that had smoke rising off it. It had to be skunk fumes.

"I hope we get called out on another call so we can leave him quickly with the jailers," said Officer Max. They pulled in at the police station and jumped out of their car to look at Simon. The ropes were just hanging over each side of the roof, and it looked like he was stuck to it.

"The smell must have melted the ropes."

The pet-napper's smile was fading because the air was no longer blowing the fumes away. He could feel sticky grease underneath him, plastering him to the roof of the car.

"The greasy gas must have glued him down!" exclaimed Officer Max as he walked around the police car.

Officer Mike grabbed Simon's arm and tried to slide him off the roof. "He won't budge."

Both police officers planted their boots deep in the dirt so they could get a good grip on him, and they pulled hard. They used all their might and pulled until he came flying off the roof right on top of them.

"Great. More skunk poop on my work uniform," grumbled Officer Max. "I'm going to have to burn this thing." He grabbed another set of gloves out of his pocket and placed them on for more protection.

"Take me somewhere where I can breathe again. Please!" Simon begged.

Officer Mike grabbed him by the arm and escorted him to his cell. The rocks crunched as he dragged his boots through the dirt. They made their way into the building and handed him off to the jailers in relief.

The jailers were not as excited to receive him. They placed their hands over their noses and escorted him to his cell quickly. They moved so fast that they started sprinting through the building, all the way through the hallway. They fell right into the cell door as they worked quickly to stuff him in with the other prisoners. They fumbled through their keys and locked the cell door as fast as they possibly could. It smelled so bad that they rushed straight outside to get some clean, fresh air.

Simon's new cellmates glared at him with faces of complete disgust, and then they all started choking on the terrible fumes coming from his body.

"What in the world did you do?" asked one of the inmates.

"I stole the wrong pet," Simon said with an embarrassed grin. They looked at him with a sick look and then they all pulled their shirts off and tied them around their faces to try and block the smell.

The day dragged by and when it was time to go to sleep, all the inmates pulled their mattresses off their beds and stuck them over their faces to block the strong fumes. Every man in the jail was rethinking the crimes they had committed.

9

Home Sweet Home!

The police headed to Simon's house the next day to see if they could find the other pets that were missing. They found a thick, blue collar lying in the gravel driveway that had Ralph's (the stolen pug) name on it. No one answered the door, so they kicked in the door in and started hunting through the house. They worked their way from room to room, investigating every corner and closet, but all they found were Coke cans and junk food lying around everywhere. But in the very back room, they found two crates sitting on a long, brown table.

"Jackpot! Both pets in one place!" yelled Office Mike.

Jewel, the turtle, was sitting in her crate with her feet and head tucked in her shell. It almost looked like there was no turtle and only a large empty shell. She was there though. Jewel was so scared, she had pulled her head and all four legs in as far as they could possibly go, and she wasn't coming out anytime soon. In the other crate, Ralph the pug was curled up in a corner. He'd been chewing on the bars, trying to get out. His mouth was puffy and sore from chewing so long. Both pet crates were labeled with signs saying they were for sale.

Officer Mike grabbed each crate and quickly loaded them up in his Range Rover. He drove right to the turtle's home first and pulled up in the long, steep driveway.

Jewel's family peeked out the window and saw him walking up the driveway with Jewel in the crate. "They found her! Jewel is home!" Katelynn cheered.

Derek, her brother, dropped his cell phone and went running out the door, with Katelynn right behind him. The screen on his phone broke, but he didn't even care. "You found her, Officer Mike! You are our hero!" Derek announced.

They grabbed Jewel and kissed her all over her shell repeatedly. She stuck her head out in excitement when she heard their voices and got a kiss right on her hard, stubby nose. She pushed her legs and tail out and started swinging them back and forth. Katelynn and Derek grabbed her and set her down in the front yard, and she started bucking up and down with excitement.

"I've never seen a turtle buck before," declared the officer with a smile.

Jewel looked like she couldn't even hold in her happiness. She had never bucked like a horse before, but she kept on jumping. The children hugged the officer to thank him for all his help and told him he was the best officer in the world. Little did they know it was Spike that had really saved the day.

Then it was Ralph's turn. He began to dance around in his crate.

"All right, Ralphy Boy! We will head to your home now," cheered the officer.

Ralph's house was straight down the street on the corner. His whole family was sitting out in the front yard, and they jumped out of their chairs when they saw the officer pull up. "It's Ralph!" they all yelled at the same time.

Ralph did flips in his crate. It almost looked like he had rabies because thick pieces of foam started forming in his cheeks. His tongue flapped from one side of his mouth to the other, and chunks of slimy, slobber flew out of his jaws everywhere. He tucked his head down and did three somersaults right in his crate.

Kim and Sarah laughed hard and reached in, pulled him out of his kennel, and hugged him close to their hearts. "I love you so much," whispered Sarah in his ear. She smiled from ear to ear and cuddled him tight. Kim scratched him behind the ears and rubbed his stomach. Ralphy was so happy, he just shook his head from side to side and reached his paws around Sarah's neck. It was a real live dog hug. Ralphy was finally home with his amazing family.

Simon the pet-napper was not as popular in jail as he was in school, and rumors spread all over the city that he was smelling up the cells. Crime was at an all-time low because people were afraid to get thrown in jail with him. As the days went by, Simon soon realized stealing pets to get money for his red race car was not the right choice. His car no longer mattered now that he was behind bars. People in jail were treating him like he had treated so many kids in school. It was a horrible feeling, and it made him realize how important it was to be kind to everyone and never think he was better than they were.

As time went by, Simon began to try to make a difference and do kind things for others. To make up for the pets he stole, he raised money on the internet for animals without homes. He collected more than five thousand dollars in one year, and he helped feed many homeless pets.

However, they say Simon still smells a little like a skunk to this day, and no one wants to sleep in the same cell with him.

Later, the town searched everywhere to try and find Lola and her exotic pet cat (secretly a skunk) to thank them for stopping the pet-napper. They'd bought dozens of presents for her, but when they finally found out where she lived, Lola, with Spike in her backpack, was already off on her next crime-fighting adventure and couldn't be found!

About the Author

Michelle Green is an elementary and middle school teacher whose favorite classes are science, technology, engineering, art, and math (STEAM). She has a master's in technology from Arizona State University, a bachelor's in education from New Mexico State University, and an associate degree in biblical studies from Charis Bible College.

She loves spending her days working with students and her evenings hanging out with her beautiful daughter and devoting time to her hobbies—drawing, writing, hiking, and riding bikes. She also enjoys spending hours on anything that has to do with technology such as coding, Photoshop, website work, creating videos, and more. You can find her cuddling with her three dogs and one cat regularly!

Write to Michelle at mycrimefightingpetskunk@gmail.com.

Acknowledgments

I would like to thank so many people. First, I would like to thank my amazing daughter Tori Sloan. Thank you for your kind heart and kind words. I also would like to thank my mother Sharon, my stepfather Bob, my stepsister Shannon, and my awesome nieces and nephews: Harper, Oriona, Zion, Jasper, and Christian. You are the best!

I would also like to thank my friends Franny, Jerry, Shelly, Stetson, Cardigan, Mina, and Becca for all your support and kindness! You were all an inspiration to me when I wrote this book too. It is friends like you who make our world a better place to live!

Most of all, I would like to thank each and every single one of my students. Thank you for all your kind words and support. You are the very reason I worked so hard to write and illustrate this book! Please remember to reach for your dreams and never give up!

www.ingramcontent.com/pod-product-compliance
Lightning Source LLC
Chambersburg PA
CBHW060355180626
46817CB00008B/3030